My Native American School

written by
Carol Gould

illustrated by
Paul Drzewiecki

KAEDEN BOOKS™

I go to the Native American school. So did my great-grandma.

At my Native American school
I do lots of things that my
great-grandma did. I play
Who Can Run To The Big Rock.

I play hide and seek
behind the rocks and hills.

I play Catch the Rabbit up
and down the hills.

I catch fish in the river.

I dance to the big drum
like my great-grandma did.

Sometimes at school I think about my great-grandma.

I am happy at my Native
American school.